SACRED FIRE

POETRY AND PROSE BY

Nancy Wood

PAINTINGS BY

Frank Howell

DOUBLEDAY

Published by Doubleday
a division of
Bantam Doubleday Dell Publishing Group, Inc.
1540 Broadway, New York, New York 10036

Doubleday and the portrayal of an anchor with a dolphin are trademarks of
Bantam Doubleday Dell Publishing Group, Inc.

Library of Congress Cataloging-in-Publication Data
Wood, Nancy C.
Sacred fire / poetry and prose by Nancy Wood; paintings by Frank Howell.
p.   cm.
Summary: A collection of poems and paintings centered on the beliefs
and ancestral wisdom of the Pueblo Indians of the
American Southwest.
ISBN 0-385-32515-0
1. Pueblo Indians—Juvenile poetry.   2. Pueblo Indians—Juvenile
literature.   3. Children's poetry, American.   [1. Pueblo Indians—
Poetry.   2. Indians of North America—Southwest, New—Poetry.
3. American poetry.]   I. Howell, Frank, ill.   II. Title.
PS3573.O595S23   1998
811'.54—dc21
97-39414
CIP
AC

The text of this book is set in 13-point Weiss.
Book design by Semadar Megged
Manufactured in the United States of America
October 1998
10 9 8 7 6 5 4 3 2 1
BVG

For CAROLYN JOHNSTON,
cherished friend, dear companion, and patient mentor,

and for ANNA GIDLEY,
sister in the wilderness,

and for FRANK HOWELL,
whose creative genius made our books possible for twenty-five years.

Cactus Flowers

The Old Man's Tale

A long time ago, yet not so very long ago, an Old Man lived in an ancient pueblo along the Rio Grande, in a part of the world now called New Mexico. He was a good spirit, perceived the way spirits usually are, in the deep silence of the night, on the gentle tongue of wind, or in solitude, when connection to a deeper world is possible. Sometimes the Indian people saw him. Sometimes not. The Old Man's job was to keep the Sacred Fire burning, so that they could remember the ways of their ancestors.

In the flame was wisdom.

In the smoke was purification.

In the ashes was potential.

Sacred Fire meant longevity and hope. It was part of the Four Great Ancestors—Water, Air, Earth, and Fire—necessary for all life. Though Coyote Brother often brought Sacred Fire to the pueblos himself, and Eagle Sister sometimes caught a piece of the Solar Fire in her beak and dropped it down, it was the Old Man who carried Fire from village to village, inside a hollowed-out stone suspended from a long pole by leather thongs. With Fire, people stayed warm. They cooked their meat. They told their stories around the smoky, glowing embers. The Old Man listened. Sometimes he gave them stories of his own to think about.

Living among them as he did, the Old Man watched the history of his people unfold. For hundreds of years they farmed the dry land, hunted game in the mountains, and developed an elaborate cosmology that connected all things into one unified, living whole. Fire—most of all the Father Sun—was the source of this great, interconnected life. The Sun's lowest point and highest point—the summer and the winter solstices—were celebrated with ceremonial dances and the authoritative beating of the drum, which, it was believed, contained the greatest stories of all. The Pueblo world was powerful and continuous, centered around the seasons, the village, and sacred rituals that celebrated corn, animals, hunting, planting, and harvest. The special wisdom of the Indians grew from countless generations of observation, the telling and retelling of ancient legends, and the worship of sacred spirits who made such a marvelous life possible. One of these spirits was the Old Man, watching, waiting, issuing warnings, at other times playing his flute or beating his well-worn drum. He knew the history, though he had his own interpretation.

After New Mexico was invaded by Spanish conquistadors in 1540, drastic change occurred. Starvation, disease, slavery, torture, and displacement took their toll. Entire villages crumbled into dust. Some Pueblo populations fled; few left clues about where they went. In less than a hundred years, the Pueblos of New Mexico changed forever. A new language, new customs, and a new religion were forced upon them. The fight was to preserve not only their lives, but also their heritage, threatened by wave after wave of fanatic priests and soldiers of the Spanish king.

Desperately, the Indian people reached out for the Sacred Fire the Old Man brought to them in the kivas, where they sang and prayed to the *katsinas*, gods who had always helped them before. If the fire went out, the people's spirit would die. That much they knew. They prayed and resisted, hid out in the mountains, fled to their Hopi relatives in Arizona, armed themselves with stolen weapons. It was too late. Whole families were marched to Mexico City to be sold as slaves. Others were forced to build huge, thick-walled churches, to grow crops for the invaders, and to hunt for them in the wilderness that the Indians knew so well. The sacred land that had nurtured and sustained them was soon claimed in the name of the Spanish king, divided up among his favorite mercenaries, and forbidden to the Pueblos, who had always hunted and worshipped there. Most of this land was never returned. Over time, highways, cities, dams, housing developments, and fences ruined it.

The Old Man saw everything. He remembered everything.

When it came time for him to tell his story, he told it. Sometimes he sat on a rock overlooking the river, where he used to live. Sometimes he walked across the desert, where he felt at home. Sometimes he went to the mountains. At other times he was adrift in the clouds. When the Pueblos revolted in 1680, destroying the churches and driving the Spaniards out of the country, the Old Man was watching. He brought Fire to them as they sought to preserve their short-lived freedom; he lighted the way when the Spaniards returned and began to make peace. He gathered Arrow Maker, Corn Planter, Deer Hunter, Storyteller, Cloud Catcher, War Chief, Mud Builder, Moccasin Maker, Bead Worker, Snake Keeper, and Pot Maker. He purified them according to ancient custom. He gave them the knowledge they would need for the struggle ahead. He sent them into the hearts of their old villages, where they remain to the present day.

This is the way it was.

NANCY WOOD
Santa Fe, New Mexico
November 1997

War Ponies

Sacred Fire

When we were driven from our homeland,
the Old Man hid the Sacred Fire
of our ancestors for safekeeping. Our bones
were weary from the grinding edge of battle.
Our minds were filled with so much confusion
we could not move from the places we had fallen.

When the Old Man blew on the embers,
a tongue of flame pierced
our center of despair. We beat our wings,
steadily, to keep the Sacred Fire alive
with the power of resistance. Day and night
we struggled to stay warm. Apprehension

melted. For three hundred years of darkness,
we held on to the light. The Sacred Fire
of existence is how we survived
the delusion that the efforts of our conquerors
last longer
than the dead arrows of our ancestors.

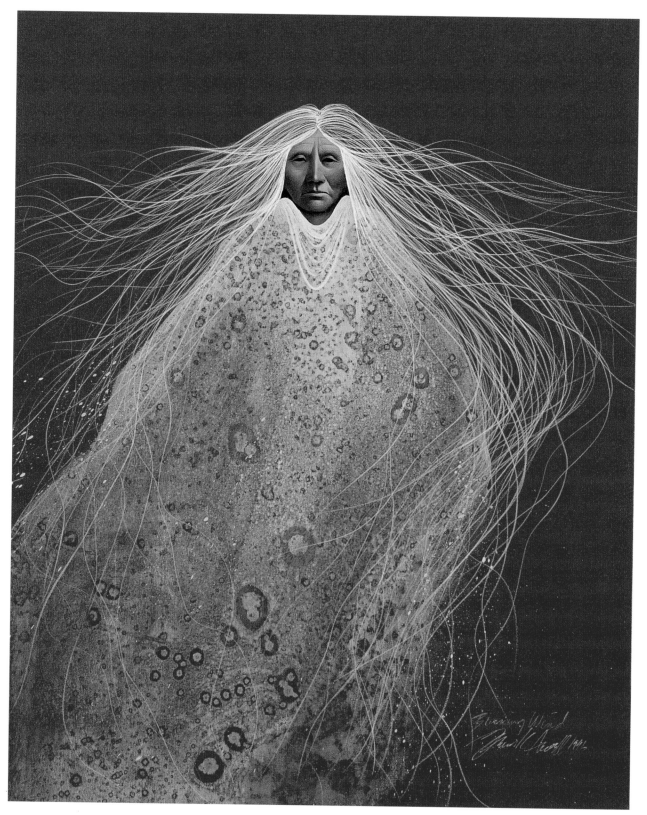

Burning Wind

The Four Gifts

I am the first spirit.
I am the last spirit.
I am eternity, said Fire.

Before me was nothing.
After me is nothing.
In between is Being, said Wind.

I am complexity.
I am simplicity.
I am balance, said Earth.

I am life.
I am death.
I am lashed to time, said Water.

In order to establish precedence in the world,
the Four Gifts became smoke, seed,
mud, and hurricane. They dwelled within
the landscape of the heart, nurturing mystery,
creating balance and eternity.

Journey

Into the place where the eagle was sleeping,
we went. Into the rock where the river
was born, we went. Into the earth
where old bones were crumbling, we went.

Into the star trails, we went. Along
the bottom of oceans, we went. New lives
grew out of salt and green moss,

And these we borrowed to make
our weak blood strong. We created
an invisible world to satisfy a visible need.

We forfeited our place in the sky
in order to be comforted
by the yellow flame
of hope.

When Earth was first made, she was empty, the Old Man says. No wind to cleanse the surface. No trees and no flowers. No four-legged animals and no songbirds. The Old Man sits on a riverbank, smoking a long-stemmed pipe. Birds and animals drop by to visit him. Fish poke their heads from the river. Leaves turn over in greeting.

Rain fell. Land rose up. Snails arrived. Then turtles. Plant Beings. Bird Beings. Animal Beings. Finally the People climbed out of the center of the Earth on a cornstalk. They settled here where we are now. In all the world there is no place like this. The People led the river down from the mountain so that it wouldn't get lost. They watched it grow accustomed to itself. Roadrunner told them to build their village out of earth. Stir in stalks of grass, he said. Feathers. Animal dung. They planted corn from seeds the Corn Mother had given them. But the People were cold, and they had no way to cook anything.

The first Being to bring Fire to the people was Coyote. He shot an arrow into the Sun and a piece of Fire fell to the ground. He carried it in his mouth to the first village. And the second. On and on. But Coyote's mouth became scorched. I was a Young Man at the time, so I walked to all the villages, with Fire safe inside a hollow stone suspended between two poles. I gave it to the ones who were worthy of it. At last the People were able to cook their food and stay warm. Fire illuminated the night. It opened people's hearts and made stories pour out. Fire is a Profound Spirit.

The Old Man looks at the river and the sky and the land. I am Keeper of the Flame, he says. As long as it burns, our knowledge is safe. In the kiva, we still have some of the original ash from the Sun's Fire that Coyote brought. Imagine. Between his hands an ember glows. He passes it to the people listening to his stories. They hold the fire, reverently, and bend closer to its flame. No one's hands are burned, but their faces glow, illuminated from within.

Visitor

The Spirits

What came with us in the Beginning Time?
    Turtle Spirit.
What comforted us in the Middle Way?
    Buffalo Spirit.
What will survive at the end?
    Earth Spirit.
What helps us to embrace old ways?
    Eagle Spirit.
What encourages us to think like animals?
    Bear Spirit.
What gives us the strength to go on?
    Human Spirit.
Who are you, gnawing at my shadow?
    A thousand spirits,
    abiding within you
Along with the wisdom of Buffalo and Eagle.

Distant Mountains

The Great God Mountain

The Great God Mountain burst from Earth's deep belly and
  lay cooling in the rain until slick grass invaded
  his rock-hard nakedness. The Great God Mountain
  swallowed meandering clouds, then devoured dying stars
  looking for a place to lie down. The Great God Mountain

Made room for rocks and trees, birds and animals, also mystery,
  necessary to sustain belief. The Great God Mountain wept
  tears enough to give birth to rivers and was patient
  during the time it took to form a perfect flower.
  What belonged there loved him. In the morning rain,

He loved them back. Trees and rocks. Birds and animals, also
  insects. But most of all the tiny flowers,
  which clung to his windswept slopes
  as if he would save them
  from the icy breath
  of winter.

Rock Drawings

If we had not left our secrets etched in stone,
we would have forgotten how to think like animals.
If we had not placed our hearts inside the rock,
we would have bled to death. In the rock are stories
of what sustained us and a prediction of what will happen
when people fail to live right. Our messages
are mysteries as deep as the sky that helped us create
a pathway to the inner life. Look at them carefully.

The Bear. The Elk. The Snake.
The Running Man. The Birthing Woman.
The Red-Tailed Hawk. The Thunderbird.
The Humpbacked Flute Player and the Warrior.

We are they. When the rocks begin to speak,
the world will know
the secrets of our time.

Animal Wisdom

At first, the wild creatures were too busy
to explore their natural curiosity until
Turtle crawled up on land. He said:
What's missing is the ability
to find contentment in a slow-paced life.

As the oceans receded, fish sprouted whiskers.
Certain animals grew four legs and were able
to roam from shore to shore. Bear stood
upright and looked around. He said:
What's missing is devotion
to place, to give meaning to passing time.

Mountains grew from fiery heat, while
above them soared birds, the greatest
of which was Eagle, to whom penetrating
vision was given. He said: What's missing
is laughter so that arguments
can be resolved without rancor.

After darkness and light settled their
differences
and the creatures paired up,
people appeared in all the corners of

Ravens

the world. They said: What's missing
is perception. They began to notice
the beauty hidden
in an ordinary stone,
the short lives of snowflakes,
the perfection of bird wings, and

the way a butterfly speaks
through its fragility. When they realized
they had something in common with animals,
people began saying the same things.
They defended the Earth together,
though it was the animals who insisted
on keeping their own names.

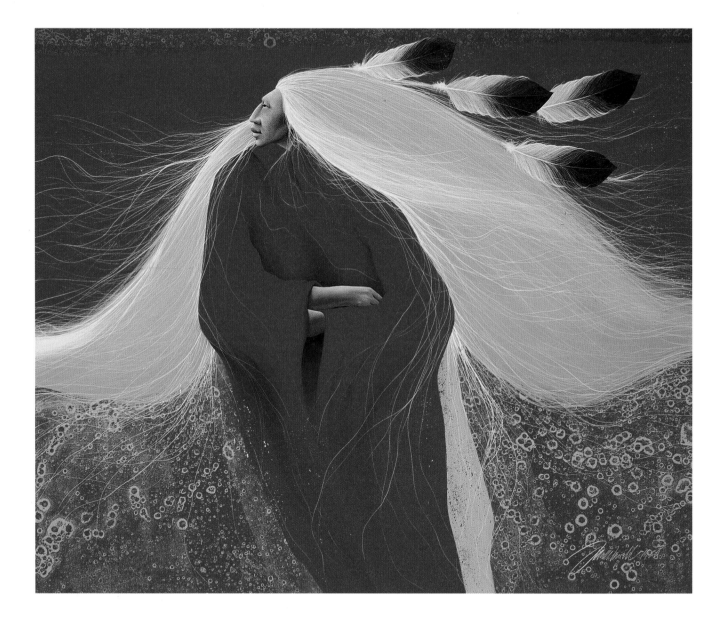

Dream Sequence—Plant Genesis #1

Creation Song

The first sounds of the Universe were footsteps,
though people were not yet made. The footsteps
went from star to star, wearing a pathway
of potential through the sky. The footsteps
brought desire, which precedes
a heartbeat waiting to be born.

The first songs arose from nothingness:
We are wing and bone,
blood and skin. We are the breath
that never dies. That was all
the Earth needed to align itself
with perfection. The footsteps
went on, and within
the mystery of creation
they gave the power of vision
to people emerging
from the inside of a flame.

Eating from the Fire

We are hungry as wolves deprived of rabbits.
Our bellies contract from emptiness, as if
we had not eaten in years. The food we crave
is rotten. Old songs in a language that died
with our horses. Old ways kept alive on a thread
of remembrance. The faces of people
who went in and out of the Earth
anytime they wanted to. We are hungry,

hungry as a dry river thirsting for rain,
hungry as a seed clamoring for Earth,
hungry as a tree in search of roots.
We eat from the Fire that burns before us,

devouring the flames as if they would satisfy
our longings. Eating from the Fire means
hunger shifts from our bellies
to our brains. We are hungry to understand
why the kindling of life burned out
when we fed it with our pain.

The Fire Spirit helped the Corn Mother into the world, the Old Man says, climbing to a rock ledge above a bustling city. It turned her into lava and she flowed out, red hot and bubbling. She scoured the land with ferocity. She purified the world. She is the greatest of the Profound Spirits. Without her, nothing is made. She came out of the Void, yet she is Light. She is movement, never stopping, though she is the Eternal Stillness. She is every woman ever born, yet she is none of them.

When people lost their Center of Being, the Corn Mother helped them find it. She brought food to the hungry. Light to all the dark places. Whenever Earth needed replenishment, she gave it. Below the Old Man, highways crisscross the land. A stream of traffic roars in all directions. Houses sprawl as far as the eye can see. Jets tear the sky in two. Their contrails remind him of the backbones of animals.

The secret is to see beauty where there is ugliness, he says. He closes his eyes and leans against the rock. He sings, softly. Right now I am back in the place of my youth. Nothing is changed. Bison are charging across the plains. Thousands of them. What a cloud of dust they make! The Earth trembles. Look, there is Crazy Horse. Geronimo. Chief Joseph. Red Cloud. The great Sitting Bull. The Corn Mother is waiting for them. Do you see her? She is a plume of smoke. The Old Man laughs and laughs.

A wreath of blue smoke encircles his head.

Study for Teton Shaman

Seekers of Unearned Wisdom

Seekers of unearned wisdom,
inhabitants of the original emptiness,
what are you doing among our people,
trying to discover our secrets of tranquillity?

You who want everything fast,
you don't have time to wait for
eggs to hatch. Sunsets take a long time
to appreciate; so do migrating geese, or
the way a leaf unfolds. Sit quietly
on a rock and feel the pulse
of Creation. Take the temperature of Earth

By placing your fingers inside her sacred body.
Let us bless you with the Circle of Life
and teach you how to sit still while moving.
You won't last long unless you forget
how unimportant
is the importance of your time.

Night Flight

The Invisible World

The People knew that nothing lasts
except Sky and Earth and Water.
They fought bravely, but starvation
intervened, and the power of the enemy
destroyed them. The People knew that bones
were important, also feathers of various kinds, and
turtle shells. These they gathered and put away,

Along with the spirits of children who had died.
The People knew they had to create
a new world, so they went into hiding.
When they emerged, they saw that Sky
and Earth and Water were not recognized
by anyone except themselves. They remained invisible,
defending their right to protect

Bones,
spirits of children,
and feathers of various kinds.

The Memory of Obsidian

We were afraid to remember obsidian,
because it reminded us of pain, so
we forgot the power of what lies behind obsidian.
We were afraid to remember eagles, because
they reminded us of freedom, so we forgot
the power of eagles and their purpose in the sky.

We were afraid of the energy of corn, because
corn was our Sacred Mother, so we
forgot our connection to corn. We were afraid
to remember bears, because they reminded us
of our lost lives, so we forgot the lessons
of Profound Beings in a world consumed by greed.

With so much forgetting, the ways of a people
were destroyed, but the power of obsidian,
> eagles,
> corn,
> and bears,
> went on.

The Old Man is talking to some visitors who have come to the village to learn the ways of his people. They make a circle around him and listen while he speaks.

Long ago, fish lived in harmony with birds, he says. Lizards spent time with fireflies. Each creature had knowledge of its own time. They shared it with one another. If the caribou put his ear to the ground, he might hear the iguana making reptilian sounds in the jungle far away. Eventually he would know about iguanas. This was how bears and owls became educated. Back and forth everything went, carrying knowledge.

When the People arrived, they brought a religion of blood, which was the same as animal blood, but different. They brought a religion of bone, which was the same as bird and animal bone, but different. A religion of harmony connected rocks and insects, birds and trees, clouds and animals. The People recognized their place in the Universe, neither above nor below, but equal. They learned the lessons of deer and badgers, rabbits and hawks, lizards and turtles, bears and crickets. After Bluebird brought them language, they were able to speak about beauty and wonder, danger and heartbreak. They added words to songs.

The People never died. They became the spirits of birds and animals. These, in turn, became human again, on and on, in a never-ending circle. When you hear a meadowlark, it's probably one of the ancestors, trying to tell you something. The trick is to listen.

The Old Man wraps his blanket around his shoulders and walks away. The people look after him. They notice that his body dissolves. A bright green toad hops across the ground where he has been walking. The toad is speaking words the people understand.

Standing Rock Women

Why the Earth Spat Fire

When the Earth calmed down
    from the long agony
    of her waterless birth,
She spat Fire, and certain possibilities emerged.
    The bones of animals,
    the fins of unborn fish, and
    the blood of scavenger birds
Were waiting for shadows to become durable
    and for dust to recognize gravity.

From the ash of Earth's spent energy
    cooling moss crept forward.
    Seas of salt ate up shorelines, and
    rock defined the essential boundaries
Of ancestry. Fire devoured
    land to make it habitable.
    All along the shores and deserts
    and mountaintops, everything
    developed eyes and hearts
    until Fire was finally satisfied.

The Fire of Memory

In the bloodred fire of memory, I see my people
burning with the knowledge of dead suns and
passion discarded by untamed stars.
Where are my people, whose land
was eaten out from under them?

In the bloodred fire of memory are chieftains
so brave they lay down with bears
and taught them
the danger of an enemy
determined to destroy
their sacredness.
Where are my people, sucked dry
by progress, yet alive to those
whose hearts perceive a deeper reality?

In the bloodred fire of memory, I hear my people
singing to preserve their attachment
to Earth and Sky. I see an eagle soaring
with a message of encouragement
and mountains emerging from decay.
Where are my people, who fought ignorance
with wisdom and created worlds beyond the obvious?

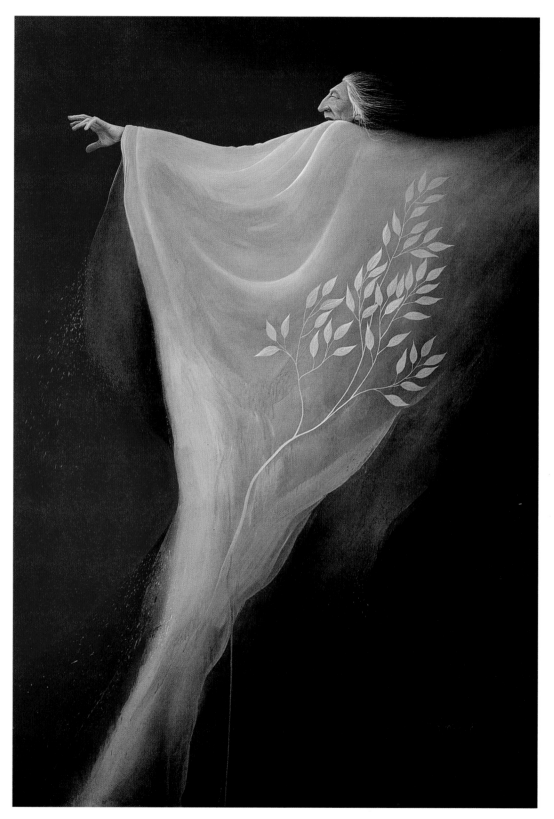

Red Flight Through Memory

They are walking.

They are burning.

They are staring.

They are raging.

They are rising.

Here, now and always,

in the bloodred fire of defiance.

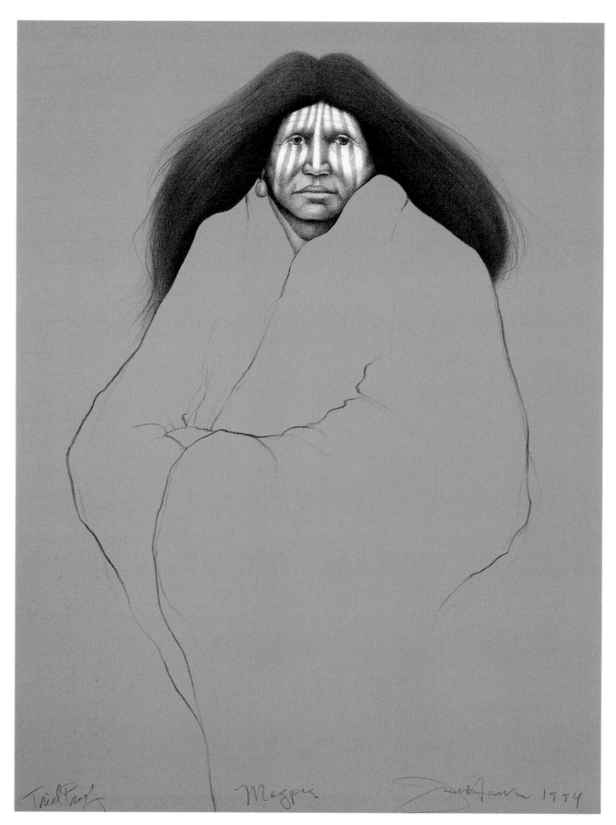

Magpie

Time's Gift

The sacred land of our ancestors bled thistles
    as it waited, in vain, for mercy. In the sky,
    the anguish of clouds stifled our holy
    dances. You were our bitter

Enemies, unwelcome in our midst, ignorant
    of Turtle language, blind
    to the beauty of our anthills,
    deaf to the chatter of piñon jays.

We killed you in our minds
    ten thousand times over,
    until we believed your downfall
    was possible, but it was only

The spreading fire of illusion.

The Memory of a People

The memory of those days of sorrow will never leave us.
How we hid like gophers, played dead
like possums, turned into the nothingness of air.
The memories of valued lives ruined
by brutish layers of authority
are cut into our brains like old markers.

The remembrance of the Earth in a perfect time
gives us both anguish and illusion. It was
the end of balance, of plenty, of stamina.
The splendor of the mountains was pulverized
into dust. The Wind lost direction because
no one sang the necessary songs.

Out of Mother Earth's navel, purifying smoke rises,
penetrating ignorance, cleansing
the filth of commerce, rising to the secret source
of springs, of sleeping seeds, of embryonic animals,
and there we find our origins.

The Old Man has been walking across a vast and mystical desert. He turns his face to the emerging Sun and reclines in the shade of a giant saguaro. A scorpion crawls up his arm. A rattlesnake coils itself around his thigh. He welcomes these friends warmly. A raven circles overhead. The Old Man and the bird speak the same language.

When the Earth was young, a great sickness came upon the people, he says. Everyone died except a small boy. One day, while he was playing, Snake bit him. The boy cried, he was in such pain. Blood came out and finally he died.

His tears became our lakes.

His blood became our mountains.

His bones became tall trees.

His spirit became flowers.

That was how Earth became.

A long time passed. One day, on a tropical island far from here, three ships arrived. The people swam out to greet them. The admiral stepped ashore and looked around. He wanted gold, but there was no gold. So he killed the people. In a very few years no people were left on that island. The admiral's name was Columbus, Bringer of Death.

The Old Man stares across the desert. He sees beneath the sand, beyond the clouds. The end of everything began with Columbus, he says. The Animal Beings died. The Plant Beings. The Bird Beings. Twenty million First People on two continents they now call America. The small boy, who was here at the Beginning Time, reappeared. This time, he was a warrior on a fine white buffalo. Through five centuries of turmoil he led his people. That's why so many of us are still connected to those times.

Untitled

When the Battle
Was Over

When the battle was over, nobody won. We lay dead,
but came to life when we heard the song of wind.
Our bones mended with the help of animals
and birds. We learned to fly on broken wings,
and to walk on crippled legs. We decided to speak lies,
so no one would learn our secrets. We pretended
to accept defeat, for guile was how we survived.

The enemy saw us without hearts, without brains.
They mistook our silence for agreement as they
stilled our voices and gave us their learning
so we could become like them.

Ancestral fire rages inside our bellies
with the intensity of the Sun. We are hungry
for our home in the wilderness,
but here we are in thin air,
with no place to plant our corn,
no place to sharpen our tools,
no place to raise our children.
        No place.

The Breath of Fire

The sacred mountains call to me when life becomes
too hard to bear
and all that stands between me and despair is
a little waterfall. With each mile I climb,
my sadness melts away
and I feel my old self returning.
The sacred mountains cure my anger
and replenish my will to resist
those who would diminish me.

In wildness, I am made whole by beauty.
In wildness, I am humbled by majesty.
In wildness, I am content to find
    eternity in a buttercup
    and courage in a drop of rain.

The Fire of Women

We are the eternal, we who have borne the pain and
grown old with only half our song being heard,
bodies aching from desire never satisfied
from mere mating with a man. We meet adversity
head-on, desiring recognition of our natural ways. We accept
the confused words of men who are strangers to our souls.

Our pulse throbs with messages from grandmothers
fooled by dreams, like us. In our bones is bred
the patience of women who stayed with men
who did not love them, and the ache of women who died
of heartbreak. Women learn from the anguish
that precedes calm, remembering how a child
bursts headlong from the womb,
and with its very first breath
begs to hear our song.

Winter Cloud

Connections

I am all things, connected to all time and all places.

    I am the undernourished bones of aged men.

    I am the new blood of unborn babies.

    I am a virgin searching for a lover.

I am a seed, waiting to become corn. I am ancient Fire,

    cleansing the ravaged Earth. I am Ice, begging for

    replenishment. I am all things, connected to

    all animals and birds. See me running with buffalo?

See me soaring with eagles? What they are, I am.

    Where they go, I have been before.

    When they die, a part of me dies also.

    When they are born, my life begins anew.

    Out of stone-cold earth, I have become a flame.

42/140   Two Women   1992

Two Women

Footsteps

Across this wounded land, where the tears
    of our ancestors made
    stillborn forests grow,
we are walking. Over this fragile earth,
    where shattered dreams
    reemerged as secrecy,
    we are walking. Up to the mesa tops,
where people became bluebirds, we are walking.
    Along the Great River,
    where ancestors listened to water songs,
    we are walking. To the villages
where our people watched momentum die, we are
    walking. Out of the dust of misery, we are making do
    with scraps. Out of our minds comes respect
    for ourselves. We are walking,
    day after day, year after year, even when
    we would rather lie down.

We lived inside our skins, remembering, remembering, the Old Man says. He is dressed in his finest deerskin robe trimmed with seashells and ermine. A Corn Dance will soon begin. There is much activity in the plaza. The Old Man is seated in the midst of the Corn Dance singers, beating an ancient drum. He sings the familiar songs of his people in the language taught to them by grandfather bears.

Everywhere we went, there they were, he says. Enemies beyond our comprehension. Beyond our prophecies. One wave after another, insisting that we give up our land, our homes, our women. The priests insisted we needed their God. They smashed our kivas, filled them up with sand, hanged our shamans in the plaza. With their last breath, people cried out the names of our ancient deities.

Across the land, warriors changed into mice and scampered away. Others became trees, so that the Spaniards would not notice them. The middle place is the heart, with veins reaching to all our sacred shrines. Many of these were destroyed too. Others remain to the present day. You can't kill what's in the blood. We knew this; the enemy did not.

The Corn Mother was responsible for whatever survived. She got into the hearts of the women and stayed there. That's where our strength comes from. The women. They go about their work with the beauty of clouds, the quietness of leaves, the wisdom of the ages. Wherever the Corn Mother went, she created new songs. She taught the People new dances. When they were starving, she taught them to eat grass. I watched her grow into a beautiful old woman. She could not be possessed by love, though she listened when I told her what was in my heart.

The Old Man's voice rises to the clouds. It is a love song for the Corn Mother.

Leaving the Body to Reach the Soul

I stand here naked, fully clothed
 in the spiritual garments of my soul.
You speak, but I hear only the murmurs
 of my drifting heart. I no longer reside
Amidst the noise and treachery
 of everyday life. I am moving toward
A new, harmonious house. As I leave my body
 to reach my soul, look for me in autumn leaves
 and moonlight, the howl of coyotes, the rush of wings.

I am the energy of roots going deep into hallowed ground
 and flowers deciding when to bloom, and rain
Becoming part of Earth. I have become you,
 waiting to find new life
 amidst the fragments of my dreams.

Night Echoes

The Old Woman's Longing

From the deep blanket of winter, I am.
From the fertile seeds of spring, I am.
From the unfolding leaves of summer, I am.
From the ripening fruits of autumn, I am.

If winter's song is one of sleep, sing it.
If spring's song is one of anticipation, sing it.
If summer's song is one of fullness, sing it.
If autumn's song is one of change, sing it.

What you are, I am.
What I am, you will be.
Where summer goes, I follow.
Where winter goes, we walk together.
The longing of this old woman
is satisfied by the loving of that old man.

Studies for Women Waiting Series

How Beauty Went On Living

My love is gone, but once she walked a pathway among
the stars and learned the language of river stones
to better understand their moods. My love is gone,
but once she danced on mountaintops and sang
with coyotes about the meaning of their lives. The sky
that claims the wide horizons of her heart

Is broadened by the wildness of her dreams. Beauty
travels with her, also the memory of sunsets and white stones.
She left an imprint of her smile upon the face of children
and whispered poems to those who didn't believe
in words. My love is gone,
but she is still the other half of the rainbow,
the deep pocket of the sea where new life forms.

We will miss her ceremonies for the Moon and her dances
to honor the sacred positions of the Sun. We accept
her inheritance of wild passion
and we honor the truths she left behind
to soothe our rage at the theft
of springtime's nurturing rain.

Lakota Crow Owner

Listening for Thunder

Oh, my dry and aching land. We do not respect you anymore.
Oh, my people, you have deserted your old ways.
We are not living as we should.
    If the purpose of life is more, we must do with less.
    If the purpose of life is less, we must let go of everything.

There is no rain. Crops are dying in the fields. The land screams out.
Our village throbs with ancient messages ignored by the young.
    Fire comes to cleanse our spirits. Why do we run from it?
    Thunder rolls in the distance. Rain will come, but not now.

Our old gods have deserted us. We are not paying attention.
Our land has been abused. We no longer heed its warning.
    Is it too late to become whole people?
    Our spirits are broken.
    Is it too late to reclaim our land?
    It has died within itself.

All we can do is go on listening for thunder.
    In vain, in vain.

The Old Man walks up a steep mountain path beside a swift, clear stream. The aspen trees have turned golden. The air is dry and crisp. For a time, after we drove the Spaniards out, life was the way it had been, he says. The Corn Mother brought rain. There was plenty of game. Together we gathered horses and gave them away. We brought the buffalo home. Animals returned from the mountains. Fish jumped out of the river. We invented deep songs. New dances. Stories about how the animals helped us during the time of revolt. We could not have done it without them. I went from village to village, carrying Sacred Fire, nothing more than the will of our people to survive.

The Old Man sits on a rock by a stream. The spirits had to be coaxed out of hiding, he says. People who had changed themselves into spiders and mice resumed their lives. The religion of our ancestors flourished once again, though a dark cloud began to form. We had come together once, but we could not stay together long. The tribes fought among themselves, worse than before. We had learned the ways of our enemies. Eaten their food. Worn their clothing. Learned their language. Adapted to their religion. Now there was sickness and hunger. Attacks by Comanches, Navajos, Apaches. The elders asked the Ones Above what to do. They knew we could never go back to the old ways.

When the Spaniards returned, some tribes were glad to see them. Others were not and they fought, bitterly. In the end, we could do nothing. So the Spaniards settled our land. Married our women. They were here to stay. We were forced to rebuild the churches we had torn down. We planted their fields, listened to their promises. But our old ways never vanished. Even to the present day. See that meadowlark? That's my grandfather. He laughs. And that pretty little squirrel? That's my grandmother.

Why Fire Resisted Rain

I have a right to live, Fire said, as Rain fell
and ate its blazing life away. I purify the land.
I am useful and persistent. Spare me.

Rain fell harder and said, I make food
possible, so you must yield to me. As Fire
sputtered to an end it cried, Don't forget,
I give warmth. Rain was not interested in

Fire's predicament. It put out the flames and
Fire soon turned to smoke. The ashes
blew away and the healing work of Earth
began
in the waiting arms of Rain.

Sky Ponies

The Earth Is All
That Lasts

The Earth is all that lasts.
We who have been asleep for years
return to plant seeds in abandoned gardens.
We summon the rain and beg for the sun
to release its energy to our care.

The Earth is all that lasts.
We who were flattened by our inability
to rise above the wreckage of the past
are eating shadows
in order to stay alive.

The Earth is all that lasts.
We who were invisible, except
to those with similar vision,
stand here possessed by our old lives.
We are unwilling to disappear from our origins.
We have replaced shame with serenity,
doubt with desire.
Our skin is bursting with new muscle.
We are one with snowmelt and with Fire.

Dakota Vision

Song for a Newborn Past

A little while we lived, not forever here,
    although we were entrusted with forever
    by our ancestors, who comforted us
    with stories that never died.

We lived surrounded by the Earth
    on six sides, but the Earth helped no one
    when we departed from our obligations.
Our people emerged in harmony and fled
    with an oath to survive complacency.

Our ancestors, rising from old river stones,
    and from the smoke of campfires,
    offered allegiance to a world of mystery,
    continuity,
    and good faith.

We, considering the alternatives,
    finally accepted.

The Fire of Life

Every day I bathe myself in light
and write my name in stars across the sky.
Every day I am the Fire of Life, burning
with the intensity of the Sun. The Wind cannot

blow away such passion, nor can Rain drown
the ash of love, knowing it will burn again.
Every day I bathe myself in light and dance

to the music that rivers make on their
way to the sea. The Earth hears my prayers
and gives my body a familiar form,
feminine in nature, strong and surviving.

Every day I write my name
in stars across the Universe: I am love.
The power of my flame
rises with the fury of my dreams.

The Demon of Progress

From our village we saw the Demon of Progress
    devouring the forests, tree by tree,
    and our life-giving rivers, bank by bank,
    and the sacred Mother Earth, piece by piece,
    and our brother creatures, bird by bird,
    bear by bear, buffalo by buffalo.

When there was nothing left of our homeland except
    the smoking ash of forests and the silt of rivers,
    we wept at the destruction of everything
    that had nourished us in our youth.

As the Demon of Progress devoured our precious world,
    the animals struggled to save themselves
    and the river tried to find a different course.
    Our people formed an energy so vast
    it covered the stricken land with
    green grass,
    corn seeds,
    and ants to do the rebuilding work.

We wept tears enough to make grass flourish, seeds to grow,
    and ants to float away when their work was done.
    Dormant rivers came to life, and one by one,

Raven Winds

the animals returned, the forest grew, and birds
began to sing the songs we were used to.

We captured the Demon of Progress and shot our arrows
   through its heart. When it was dead,
   we planted flowers
   where its gaping mouth had been.

An April Voice

How the Universe
Doubled

The doubling of the Universe took place when people
    were sleeping, except for a few old women
    who remembered how passion was created
    to save the world from boredom. In dresses
    made of spiderwebs, those old women

Sang a love song, heard from star to star and tree to tree,
    even from fish to fish and blossom to bee.
    Those who were in tune with one another
    responded, and those who were not
    slept their lives away. As the old women

Watched, the heat of love expanded, on and on, with colors
    so bright they singed the edge of indifference
    in one night. The Universe doubled
    with the passion of those old women,
    who believed the power of their feminine selves
    would overcome
    the doubtful hearts of men.

The world changed into something we did not recognize, the Old Man says. It was as if Earth's heart turned inside out. Blood everywhere. The stench of progress. We learned their language. Were given their names. Learned to read and write. Hunted game for them without the proper ceremony. We were forced to give up our share of food. We wept as our families were sold into slavery. We never saw them again. But, you see, people will hang on to the wind if they have to. The human spirit is the last to die.

The Old Man is lying on top of a cloud. Other clouds come by to greet him. With the most promising clouds, he discusses rain. With others he talks about what they have seen on their journey. The secret of survival is to be in two places at once, he says. When the Americans sent us to boarding school, we remained in our cornfields. When they filled our ears with a new language, we were listening to Corn Dance songs. We discovered clever ways to survive. Rocks and trees and clouds translated our missing way of life. As one circle died, a new one formed. That's what our religion is all about.

Our religion is what we do every moment of the day, like breathing. We are in touch with the largest and the smallest spirits simultaneously. It's hard work, impossible to learn in one lifetime. There are guidelines for well-ordered living. Beliefs that have held us together since the Beginning Time. You can change the world with machines that go faster than birds or animals. Tear up Mother Earth until her guts hang out. Poison the rivers and the air. Build more shopping malls. Pave more streets. Eliminate birds and animals that get in the way. Destroy forests and deserts and swamps.

What will you have in the end?

Daughters of the Earth

Daughters of the Earth, your path is strewn with stones
sharp enough to sever determination from your bones.
Nothing is as it should be anymore. Our hearts
are on the ground. Our inheritance is shattered.

Daughters of the Earth, your spirit is in danger
of suffocation. Old ideas will crush it. Indifference
will rob your house of meaning. Men are deaf
to your songs, but you must sing them anyway.

Daughters of the Earth, wisdom will save you
from being swallowed by conformity. Do not grieve
for the world of your ancestors,
but create a new horizon from the gifts
they left on the pathways of your mind.

Eagle Wing

Strengthen the Things That Remain

Rainbows still live in the sky and green grass
is growing everywhere. Clouds have familiar shapes
and sunsets have not changed color in a long time. Thunder
still follows lightning and spring comes after winter's misery.

A tree is still a tree and a rock is still a rock. A warbler
sings its familiar song and coyotes howl
in disconcerting harmony. Grasshoppers still hop

to their own music,
bees still buzz with excitement, and squirrels
still jump like acrobats. Mountains still contain mystery
and oceans surge with eternity. Bears still sleep in winter

and eagles fly higher than other birds. Snakes have an affinity
for the ground, while fish
are content in water. Patterns persist,
life goes on, whatever rises will converge.

Do what you will, but strengthen the things that remain.

Lakota Shirt Wearer

Dead Village Rising

We blessed the corn and blessed the pumpkin seeds,
    gathered salt and fed Mother Earth's navel,
    as we have done since the sacred animals
    became human. We whispered secrets
To those entrusted with the future and dressed
    ourselves in hunting clothes. We danced
    for Deer, Eagle, Buffalo,
    Butterfly, and Squash, mending circles
    broken by ignorance of sacred law.

We lived as one, yet lived as many, rejoicing
    in a balanced time that quickly passed,
    yet did not pass. We died from grief,
    yet went on living. Our wounded spirits guard
Firm memory. Our bitter hearts line the pathway
    to understanding. We are gone,
    yet in our abandoned village,
    ancestral corn is thriving.

Oglala Women

Forgetting

Forget where you came from. It is not important.
Forget your friends. They will not be with you
at the end. Forget your parents. Their job is done,
so honor them by capturing endurance,
the means by which they stayed alive.

Forget the color of sky. Where you are going requires
a different perception. Forget your name. It limits you
as a human being related to the animals. Forget love,
for it will distract you as you walk along the edge.
In starting over, embrace the flame of
nothingness. Forget possibility. It goes hand in hand
with hope. Forget that achievement matters.

Forget that others have hurt you or that life
did not give all that you deserved. Forget
your face, your voice, your intellect.
Forget those years of happiness.

Now, you are truly free.

INDEX OF TITLES